Once upon a time, there was a little bunny named Ruby.
She wore a red hood so everyone called her Ruby Riding Hood.
One day, Ruby Riding Hood decided to take Grandma a basket of cookies.

1

On the way to Grandma's house, she met the Big Max Wolf.
He was very hungry. He reached for the basket.
"Cookies!" said the Big Max Wolf.

Just as he was about to grab the basket, Ruby Riding Hood pulled it away.
"I'm sorry," said Ruby Riding Hood. "These cookies are for Grandma."
And away she went.

Ruby Riding Hood walked through the forest.
After a while, she got tired and decided to rest by a tree.

Ruby Riding Hood didn't realize that
the Big Max Wolf had followed her.

The Big Max Wolf reached toward the basket.
"Cookies!" said the Big Max Wolf.

Just as he was about to grab the basket, Ruby Riding Hood pulled it away.
"I'm sorry," said Ruby Riding Hood. "These cookies are for Grandma."
And away she went.

Ruby Riding Hood stopped at the playground.
She put the basket at the bottom of the slide
and played on the swing.

Ruby Riding Hood didn't realize that the
Big Max Wolf had followed her again.

The Big Max Wolf climbed to the top of the slide.
He slid down and reached toward the basket.
"Cookies!" said the Big Max Wolf.

Just as he was about to grab the basket, Ruby Riding Hood pulled it away.
"I'm sorry," said Ruby Riding Hood. "These cookies are for Grandma."
And away she went.

The Big Max Wolf watched Ruby Riding Hood skip away.
He was very hungry, but he did not know how to get the cookies.

Then the Big Max Wolf had an idea.
While Ruby Riding Hood talked to the woodcutter…

…the Big Max Wolf took a shortcut to Grandma's house!

He put on Grandma's shawl and waited in the kitchen.

Ruby Riding Hood arrived at Grandma's house.
"Hi, Grandma. Would you like to try some
of the cookies I made?" she asked.

Grandma reached toward the basket.
"Grandma, what funny-looking ears you have!"
said Ruby Riding Hood.

Grandma grabbed the basket.
"Grandma, what dusty little hands you have!"
said Ruby Riding Hood.

"Cookies!" said the Big Max Wolf.

Just then, the real Grandma walked into the room.
The Big Max Wolf hid behind the shawl.
"Hi, Ruby. You brought me cookies!" said Grandma.

Ruby Riding Hood looked at Grandma.
Ruby Riding Hood looked at the other Grandma.
"But how can there be two Grandmas?" she asked.

The Big Max Wolf threw off the shawl.
"Max! Or should I say the Big Max Wolf!"
laughed Ruby Riding Hood.

Grandma looked in the basket.
"Well, there's plenty for everyone.
We can all have some delicious…"

"Cookies!" said the Big Max Wolf.